Anna Obiols & Subi

Brachiosaurus

The largest dinosaur

BARRON'S

I have a friend.

He is very, very large.

He can weigh up to 99,000 lbs.

(45,000 kilograms)!

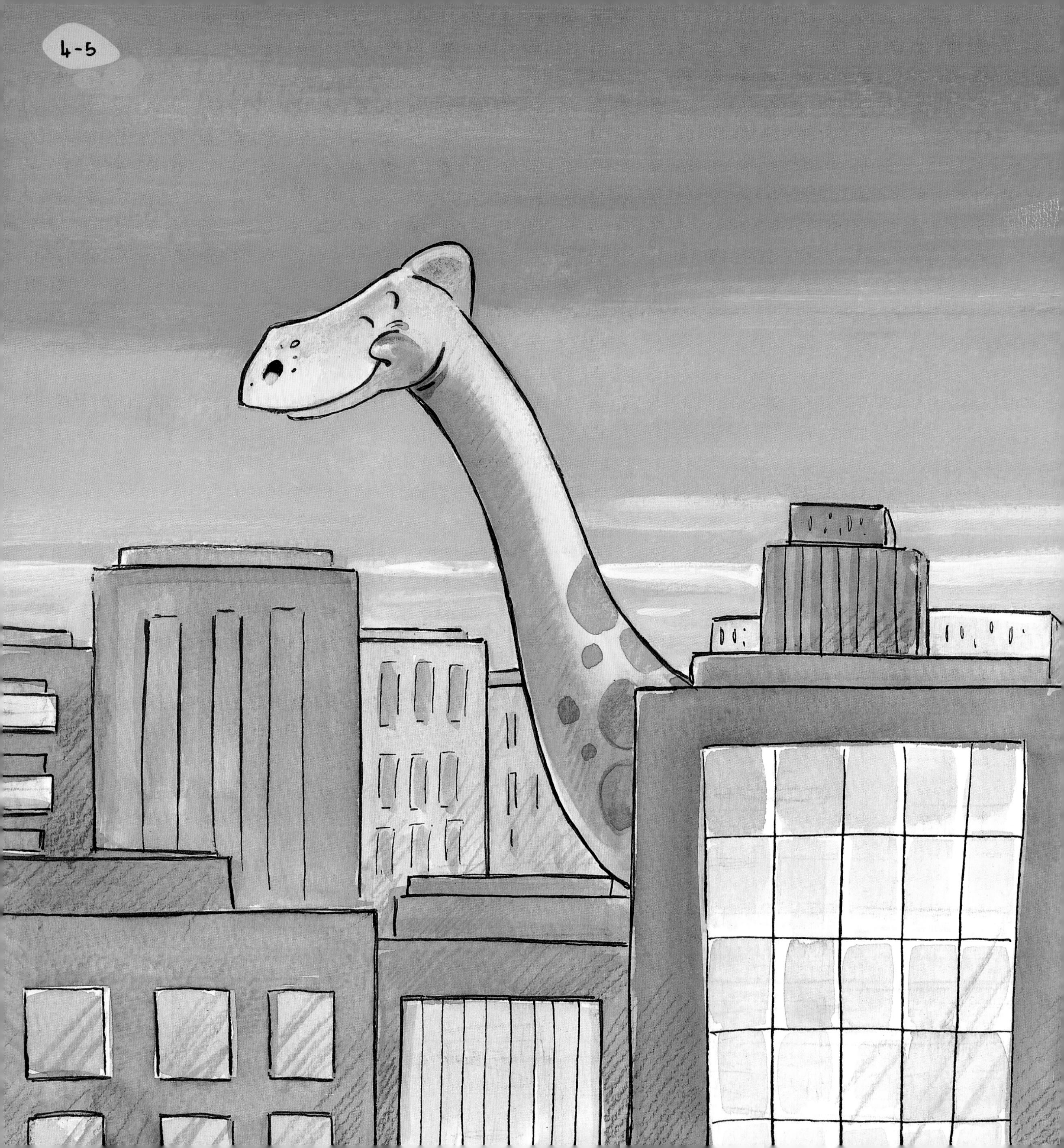

He is very, very tall.

Much taller than a skyscraper.

He has a really long tail, but it isn't a slide.

He eats lots and lots of grass. He eats more than twenty cows put together.

If you had to make clothes for him, you would need a lot of cloth and thread.

And it takes my grandmother a whole winter
to knit him a good scarf.

He is closer to the stars and the moon
than we are. And he is lucky enough to have
his head above the clouds.

If you have to wash him, don't try to put him in the bath in your house. He won't fit.

You'll have to build a special bath just for him.

If his head itches, you'll find it difficult to help
him unless you have a ladder as high as the
firemen's.

When the school bus breaks down, it's great because my friend takes us.

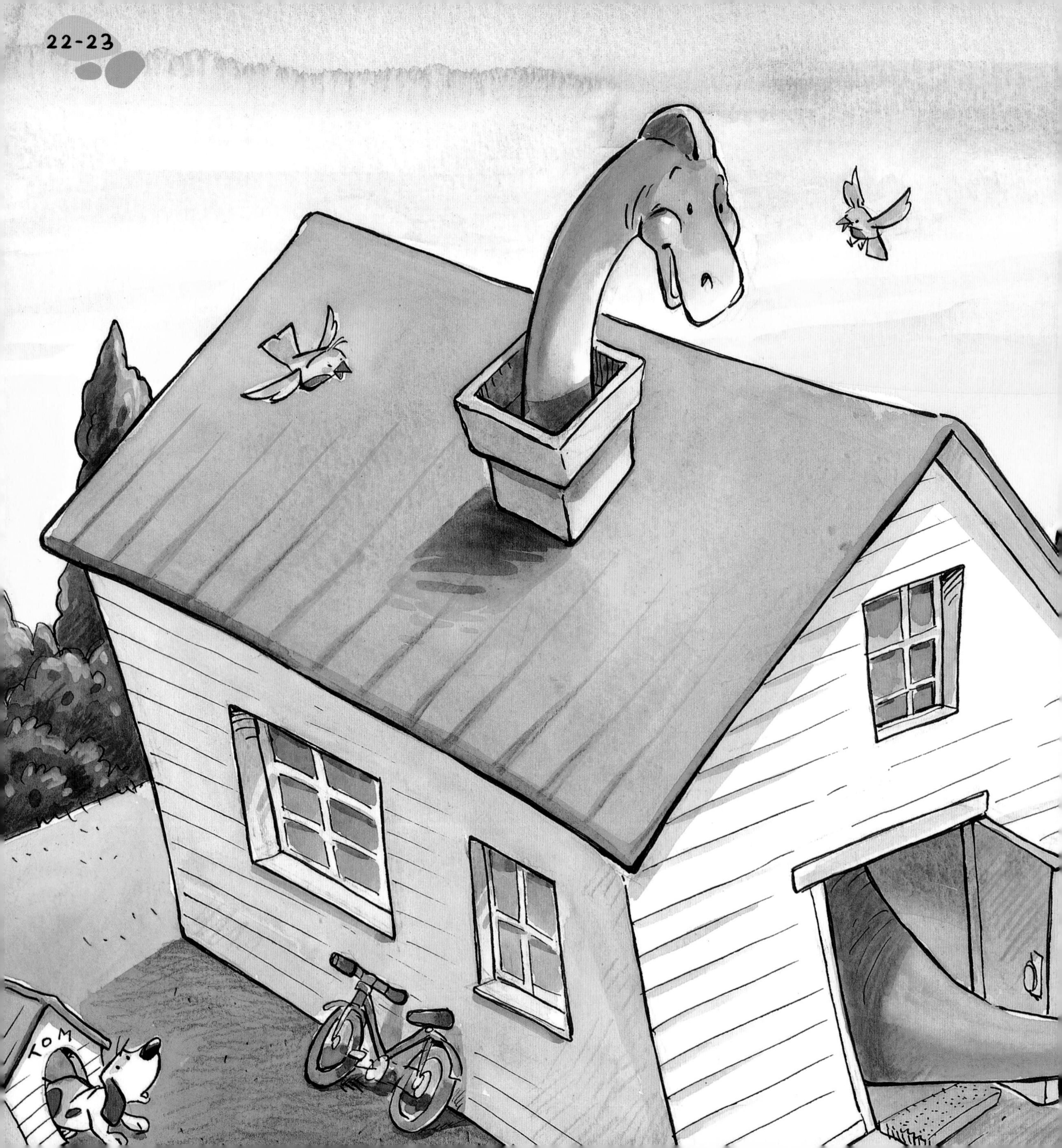
TOM

He won't fit into my house, or those of my friends.

It's also very hard to find a chair
the right size for him.

Do you know who my friend is?

The BRACHIOSAURUS that
sleeps with me every night.
Good night!

Its nose was
on the top
of its head.

It had a small,
curved head.

The Brachiosaurus

Its front legs were longer than
its back ones. (It was the only
dinosaur with legs like these.)

It had a very long neck.
It looked like the modern
day giraffe.

Its back was
curved like
that of giraffes.

It could reach 52 feet
(16 meters) high and 83 feet
(25 meters) long and could
weigh up to 80 tons.

It had a large,
long tail.

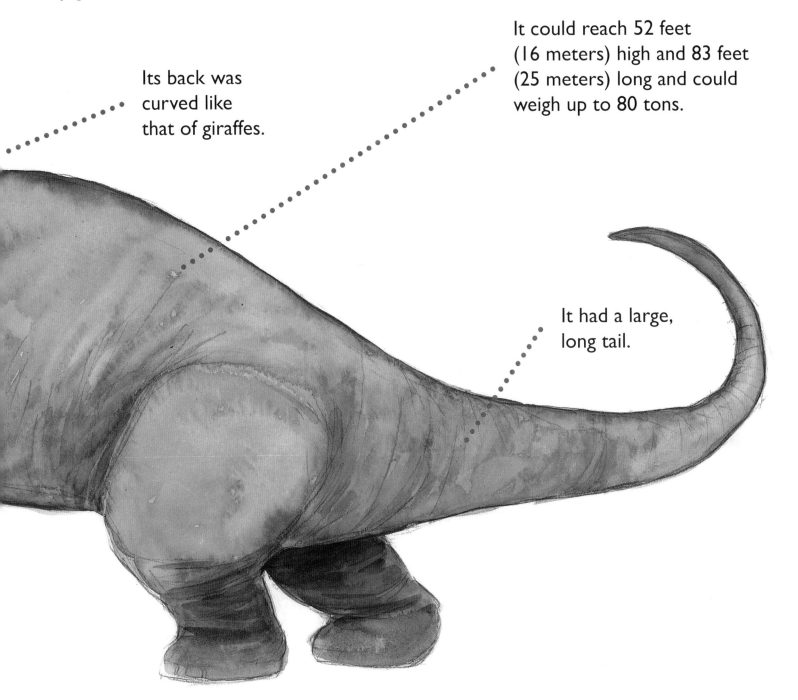

SCIENTIFIC DESCRIPTION OF THE BRACHIOSAURUS

Its name means "reptile with branch arms." The brachiosaurus lived during the Jurassic period, between 205 and 135 million years ago. During this period, there were two large continents: one in the north and the other in the south, separated by a huge sea. It was very hot, the humidity level was very high, and there were big forests.

CHARACTERISTICS

The brachiosaurus was one of the largest animals that has ever walked on the Earth. It could reach 52 feet (16 meters) high and could weigh up to 80 tons. Each bone in the back of the brachiosaurus measured 3.3 feet (1 meter) long. Imagine how large this dinosaur could be.

Its heart was very large and heavy, its brain was very small, its teeth were flat-shaped, and it used its very long tail to defend itself.

The brachiosaurus was also easily recognized, because its nose was on the top of its head. Some scientists claim that it could breathe while eating. For a long time, it was believed that the brachiosaurus spent a large part of its time in the water, thanks to the nose on its head; but today it is thought that the brachiosaurus lived only on land.

As a plant-eater, it spent most of its time eating. It is believed that it could eat 440 lbs. (200 kilograms) of plants every day.

It is known that the brachiosaurus lived in groups and that it moved from one region to another in search of food, from meadows covered in ferns to forests.

Scientists have said that it could live about 100 years, and it is known that it lived in the areas that are now North America and Africa.

FUN FACTS:

● An asteroid was given the name "9954 BRACHIOSAURUS."

● A model of a brachiosaurus skeleton has been on display
since the year 2000 in Hall B, Terminal 1 of United Airlines at O'Hare
Airport in Chicago. Another identical model, this time in bronze, is
at the Field Natural History Museum in Chicago.

● The first brachiosauruses were discovered in 1900
by Elmer S. Riggs in western Colorado.

General information about Dinosaurs

Their name means "terrible, powerful lizard" or "big reptile." The dinosaurs were a highly varied group of animals that lived on the Earth millions of years ago. The era in which they lived is divided into three great periods: the Triassic, the Jurassic, and the Cretaceous. Everything we know about these creatures is thanks to fossils, which are the remains of plants and animals that lived many years ago and have turned into stone. Thanks to these fossil remains—such as bones, footprints, skins, and eggs—we know what the dinosaurs ate, how they moved around, and how they were born. Paleontologists are scientists who study fossils. When they find the remains of a dinosaur, the first thing they have to do is dig them up very carefully. Then, all the material is sent to the laboratory, to prevent it from being damaged. The fossils are often wrapped in plaster,

which is what doctors do when they set broken legs in a cast. Later on, all the remains are cleaned and, finally, the skeleton is assembled as if the bones were pieces of a puzzle. Some of these skeletons can be seen in different museums around the world.

Thanks to scientists, we now know that dinosaurs hatched from eggs like modern day birds and reptiles. Their skin must have been rough and very thick, similar to that of crocodiles. However, we don't know what color their skin was. We also know that some of them fed on plants and others ate meat. Some walked on two legs, others walked on four legs, and others could walk either on two or four legs. Although they are known because many of them were very big, some dinosaurs were the same size as a man or even smaller.

Brachiosaurus

First edition for the United States and Canada published in 2012 by Barron's Educational Series, Inc.

© Copyright 2011 by Gemser Publications, S. L., El Castell, 38, 08329 Teià, Barcelona, Spain

Author: Anna Obiols
Illustrator: Subi (Joan Subirana)
Design and layout: Gemser Publications, S. L.

All inquiries should be addressed to:
Barron's Educational Series, Inc.
250 Wireless Boulevard
Hauppauge, NY 11788
www.barronseduc.com

ISBN: 978-1-4380-0106-7
Library of Congress Catalog Number: 2011938891

Date of Manufacture: June 2012
Manufactured by: Discovery Printing Co. Ltd, Dongguan, Guangdong, China

Printed in China
9 8 7 6 5 4 3 2 1